I0538338

falling over

A One Night Stand Novella

.melody jones

Falling Over, A One Night Stand Novella
© 2017 Melody Jones

All Rights Reserved

ISBN: 978-0-9983210-3-5

This book is a work of fiction. Names, characters, places and incidents are products of the author's imagination or used fictitiously. Any resemblance to actual persons, living or dead, or events is entirely coincidental.

Except for use in a review, no part of this book may be reproduced in any form or by any electronic or mechanical means, without the expressed, written permission of the author.

Cover Artwork: ©Sarah Hansen, Okay Creations
Formatting: Champagne Formats
Editor: Lisa Murray

For Leanne:
Thank you for 40+ years of friendship.
I'm humbled and grateful.

one

MY HEAD BANGS AGAINST THE passenger window with an embarrassing thud. The glaring rays of the sun pouring through the glass pound my eyelids, willing them to remain closed, as the rhythmic sound of the truck's engine lulls me back to sleep. "Wake up, sleepyhead," Courtney laughs from the front seat.

"I think the sun knocked me out," I state with little conviction.

"You're going to need all the rest you can get. Another hour and we will be on the lake. Are you ready to get down and crazy?" Courtney hollers loudly while displaying her best car seat dance moves.

"Let's do this!" I respond with my best contrived enthusiasm.

Settling back into my seat, I attempt to give myself a colossal pep talk. I'm turning over a new leaf, leaving all the lame-ass guys in my past. This is going to be a fun-in-the-sun weekend. A persistent ache in my belly wills me into a negative state, a sense of foreboding tries to overcome my false good mood. Nope. Not allowing any negativity to invade my brain this weekend. My hand naturally fondles the turquoise gem hanging around my neck. I wear it when I feel as though I can't dispel the negative energy hovering over me, suffocating every last positive vibe from the depths of my soul. Striving to clear my mind, I rub my finger over the surface of the stone, concentrating on the ridges and veins of the tumbled blue gem.

This is a weekend of fun, freedom, and no worries or stress. A carefree weekend on the lake with my best friend, Courtney, and her husband, Ryan. The last time I came to the lake with Courtney was two years ago, and the embarrassment of that trip is a stark reminder of what lies ahead.

I'm desperately afraid of falling over the side of the boat, and because of that, I must wear a life vest every second the boat engine is running, without question. I have a recurring nightmare where I'm on a speed boat having the time of my life, and then I fall overboard, hitting my head on the side of the boat in the process, drowning before anyone realizes what has happened. The funny part though, is I have been on a boat exactly five times in my life. An obsessive fear, yes, but a fear rooted from reality nonetheless. If it means I have to wear a life vest, then I'm fine with it. It's when other people, other boaters, realize my problem and use it as comedic fodder, turning me into a joke for every intoxicated lake-goer within hearing distance. The trauma over my last lake trip kept me away for two years, but I'm ready to try again. I'm ready for a weekend away from life. Away from men, work, and my problems.

What kind of problems could a single twenty-five year old girl possibly have? In the grand scheme of life, I'm blessed with a good family, friends, a challenging career, and I'm not ugly. But I have terrible taste in men. For the most part, I have been treated well. The problem is, I pick guys who never put me first. Sure, in the beginning, we are inseparable. The guy treats me well, takes me out, texts me during the day. As per usual, that slows down over time, and I find myself the last person on that guy's list. I bend over backwards trying to be accommodating, trying to please the guy, while easily ignoring that he just isn't that into me. I'm the girl who falls over any guy who even remotely seems appealing, going out of my way to treat a man the way I want to be treated, with trust, compassion, and caring. I fawn over them, make them their favorite meals, bake their favorite cookies, stock my fridge with their favorite beer and snacks. All the while, I'm just a blip in their day.

Drew is my latest mistake. Don't get me wrong. He's a nice guy and never treated me with disrespect, but he wasn't over the moon for me. I surmise it's easy for a guy to stay with me – I'm the perfect girlfriend who allows them to walk all over me with little fuss. After a year with Drew, I decided I had enough of the relationship. He didn't seem terribly bothered when I broke up with him, but even if he was, it was too late for me to give him another chance. In the past I may have given him other chances to be better, but I'm done with that behavior. I'm done allowing myself to be used as a doormat. Ugh, men.

Throwing myself into work the last two months has been great for my sales numbers but dreadful for my mind. Doing nothing but working has turned me into a terrible bore. Courtney, being my BFF, can't stand to see me this way and orchestrated a hostile takeover of my weekend. So here I am in the backseat of Courtney's and Ryan's extremely large truck on my way to the lake for a weekend of fun.

Courtney and I have been best friends since freshman year of high school. She is the quintessential popular girl: blonde hair, blue eyes, outgoing, athletic, and naturally beautiful. I'm her cute, not as outgoing, but sociable, best friend. Together we click. I don't know why, but I'm grateful for our enduring friendship. Her husband, Ryan, is a good guy who treats her with kindness and respect. When the two first began dating in college, I was skeptical of Ryan's motives – I thought he was like every other hot college athlete who was looking for a short-term hottie to warm his bed. He has certainly proven me wrong and then some. How could I say no when they banged on my front door at the crack of dawn and insisted I go with them to the lake this weekend?

The momentum of the truck changes, shifting my body forward at the decrease in speed. Checking out the window, I see we are exiting the highway. It appears remote and desolate – the landscape nothing more than dirt with sporadic low-lying brown shrubs – however, I know better. The wondrous and varied landscape of Arizona always holds surprises. Five miles after exiting the highway, the river that feeds the lake begins to appear. The mountains grow taller and redder the farther we travel. Another few minutes and we enter the trailer park and marina where Ryan and Courtney own a mobile home. The sun's rays warm my skin as I exit the truck and stretch the kinks out of my legs. *Be positive*, I keep telling myself. This will be a fun, relaxing weekend with great friends.

Courtney and I head inside to unpack our bags and begin to collect our gear for the day of boating ahead. It's surprising how much stuff you need to bring to enjoy a few hours on the boat. Of course, my life vest is front and center on our pile of beach towels and flip flops and bags. I hear another truck pull up outside and peer out the window. A guy hops out of the truck and greets Ryan with one of those one-armed bro hugs.

"Who is that talking to Ryan?" I ask Courtney, curious about the good-looking man on the other side of the window.

"It must be Tyler. He's joining us for the weekend," she calls from the back bedroom.

"Why don't I remember him from your wedding?" I holler over my shoulder.

"He was definitely there. Maybe you were too busy paying attention to your date – what was his name?"

"Trent," I say to the window. Another mistake I would love to forget; but of course, he is memorialized forever in the party pictures from Courtney's wedding. I'm never taking a boyfriend to a wedding again.

"That's right. He was the real estate agent who never put down his phone. I still don't know what you saw in that guy – total bore if you ask me," Courtney says over her shoulder.

She's correct on so many levels. Trent rarely had time for me – thank goodness that relationship only lasted a few months. Seriously, what is wrong with me? I'm beginning to think I only attract narcissists with commitment problems.

"Stop thinking, Emma. Everyone dates a loser once in a while. Focus on having fun this weekend and promise me you will not accept any dates or phone numbers while you are here. We are not looking for a boyfriend for you. Got it?" Courtney glares at me like I ate the last piece of pizza, and she didn't get a slice.

"Ok, I get it. You don't have to worry about me. I'm done with men for now. I'm done chasing them. The next guy I date will have to chase after me," I say with determination, looking Courtney square in the eyes.

"That's my girl," Courtney says, holding out her hand for a high-five.

I smack her hand harder than she was expecting, and we start laughing at each other.

"No more guys. Only one-night stands or a sex buddy," she says while picking up her boat bag and slipping on her sunglasses.

I laugh at her joke. At least I think she is joking. She's out the door before I can inquire further. Sex buddy, definitely not. But a one night stand? That sounds like a good idea. No expectations or commitment – I can definitely do that. Wait, that's a terrible idea, isn't it? I wouldn't say my boyfriends sucked in bed, but they certainly weren't reason to write home about. I wouldn't mind having someone handle me in that department. No more thinking. Fun. This is about having fun. Pulling my bag over my shoulder, I extract my sunglasses from the bag and head out into the sunshine.

two

COURTNEY INTRODUCES ME TO TYLER, WHO also has no recollection of meeting me at the wedding either. The four of us walk over to the marina that is attached to the trailer park. Tyler pulls a wagon loaded with an ice chest and our gear piled on top, while Ryan carries a smaller cooler. We arrive at the boat slip and make quick work of loading all our gear, putting up the bimini, and stowing all the boat stuff – that's a technical term for slip lines, buoys, and all this other junk needed to have a boat. Whatever, I'm just here for the drinks and sun and fun.

Nobody says a word when I slip on my life vest,

crack open a beer, and quietly take my seat in the rear of the boat. I surmise Ryan must have mentioned my problem to Tyler because usually by now, somebody has given me crap about the vest. My concerns about this trip start to subside. I feel the knot in my stomach beginning to untangle. Ryan cranks the motor to life, and the gentle purr of the engine is rather comforting at this point. As the vessel begins to ease backward out of the slip, Tyler jumps onto the bow from the dock just before the boat clears it entirely. Based on the confidence of his movements, it is obvious that Tyler has been on a boat more than a handful times. Mental note that Tyler may be helpful to me later in the day, in case I have any nautical-type questions or whatever.

I'd like to believe I can face my fears with strength and confidence, but sadly that's not going to happen. The farther we get from the marina into the open lake, the shorter my breaths become and the faster my heart beats. Distracting myself, I reach into the small cooler at my feet and remove a bottle of water. Gulping down half the bottle, I proceed to squeeze the life out of the plastic cylinder. The squeaky noise of the plastic distracts me from our distance to shore. *Think positively.* I've done this before and survived without a scratch to my body. Switching back to my beer, I chug the remaining liquid with fluid grace. I try to brush off the fear invading my brain. Courtney glances back at me, so I give her a thumbs up to momentarily appease her worry.

As the boat approaches the end of the no-wake zone, my stomach turns over and over in fear. My eyes are closed when I feel someone's arm squeeze me tightly. I open my eyes to find Courtney sitting on the seat next to me, a gentle smile gracing her lips. She pats my leg with her other hand. Tyler has moved into Courtney's chair next to Ryan, so I focus on his face as a distraction from my surroundings. His hair is sandy brown with a slight curl where it touches his ears. He has a strong jaw line with thin lips and a nose proportional to his face. I concentrate on the movements of his mouth as he chats with Ryan – the noise from the engine and water slapping the sides of the boat prevent me from hearing what they are saying.

"Here we go," Ryan calls out to his passengers as he turns the brim of his hat backwards and presses the throttle forward.

The engine noise increases twofold as the

propeller pushes the boat out of the water onto the surface. When we are passed by other boats headed in the same direction, I know Ryan is taking it slower than normal for my benefit. We are like the little old lady in the slow lane, holding up traffic, garnering the finger from impatient commuters. After a few minutes, my heart rate begins to ease, and I'm able to take a deep breath. My fingers have ceased their assault on my water bottle as well. I smile at Courtney, giving her thigh a gentle squeeze, and she releases my shoulders from her comforting embrace.

I have found that the best way to calm my rattled nerves is to focus on the beautiful scenery. The lake is surrounded by stunning terrain. Mountains of red rock hover on the horizon to the west. To the east are miles of rolling desert hills, with large patches of reeds hovering at the edge of the water. A wild burro stands near the shoreline contemplating a drink of water, as the rest of his pack lingers atop the hill. Despite my fear of falling out of the boat, I love the lake and its natural treasures.

After what feels like hours, the boat slows, and Ryan steers us into a small natural harbor. Several other vessels are anchored, preparing for the throng of boats that will no doubt join us over the next few hours. This is the part of the trip I enjoy—floating in the water, having a cold drink, and chatting with friends and strangers alike. Despite the nagging feeling in my stomach that something bad is going to happen, I'm glad I let Courtney and Ryan drag me out here.

The boys take care of the boat stuff, I guess. There is an anchor and buoys and ropes to be tied. I don't keep track of what they call everything, I just stay out of their way. Late spring weather is the best at the lake. The water isn't too warm yet, but it's not cold by any stretch of the imagination. Mid-day weather hovers near one hundred degrees, which is a blessing considering midsummer temperatures can reach up to one hundred twenty, and everything you touch feels like it's on fire.

Courtney and I collect our floats and not-so-gracefully jump into the water from the rear swim deck. The comforting pressure of the water on my skin helps the last bit of anxiety release from my body. Kicking my feet quietly, I settle into my float which is like a pool noodle but twice as thick. I hang my arms over the top and settle the noodle directly under my chest.

"Hey, Ryan!!" I yell. "Can you hand us a couple of Mangoes?" He looks at me and rolls his eyes. Ryan is a beer drinker, plain and simple. He can't fathom drinking one our favorite fruity drinks. Hard Mango Lemonade is the perfect drink for a cool dip in the lake- refreshing, fruity, and it doesn't make you quite as bloated as beer does.

"And can you pour it into my disco ball, please? It's right there next to your hand," I say loudly. Ryan shakes his head but completes my request. He hands me the disco ball tumbler filled with mango goodness and passes Courtney a water.

"What's up with your drink?" I question. "It's not like you to pace yourself." Courtney can certainly hold her alcohol, so her beverage choice is intriguing.

"I have a lingering stomach issue that I don't want to aggravate while we are here in the middle of nowhere," she says awkwardly. "Don't worry about me, Emma," she says, while splashing water toward me with her hand. "I'll catch up to you later. Just taking it slow this morning."

"You better catch up," I say in mock horror. "So, what's up with Tyler? He doesn't talk much. I still have no recollection of meeting him at your wedding." His face is completely foreign to me.

"Tyler is great, maybe a bit on the quiet side, but don't let him fool you. He is a major player," she says with amusement. "He has confidence sweating from every pore and then some, but his personality is on or off, nothing in between. He's not for you, Emma. No more men. Only one-night stands or eye candy."

I roll my eyes knowing she's correct. Here I am investigating any available guy as a potential mate, falling back into my comfortable patterns.

"How does he know Ryan?"

"He's one of Ryan's childhood friends. Plus they do a little work together from time to time. Ryan has helped him oversee a few of his larger residential construction projects. "

"Tyler's in construction?" I ask, still curious.

"He's the owner of a small construction firm. He runs the show but doesn't really do any hammering or that sort of thing. I don't want to talk about Tyler. What's up with you lately?" The crease in her brow sharpens as though she is preparing to strike. I ignore it for the time being, hiding my eyes behind the welcome tint of my sunglasses.

"Same stuff. Just working- trying to make the gold level sales award for this quarter. Nothing mind-blowing," I say.

"Sounds like you could stand getting your mind blown," she laughs.

"I'm a nice girl," I insist with a straight face. We both laugh because while I am a nice girl, I could definitely stand to have my mind blown by a pleasant but forcefully gentle man.

I turn to Tyler who is still in the boat chatting with Ryan.

"Another Mango, please," I tease. When they ignore me, I get louder. "Boys! Another Mango, please." They laugh in unison, and I wonder if it's at me or something they are talking about. Ryan takes my empty tumbler and refills it with fresh mango goodness. I turn back to Courtney and notice the harbor has collected quite a crowd of boats, at least forty by my estimation. I can see at least five or six more coming around the bend, as well.

"Who wants to jump?" I ask nobody in particular. The guys stare at me for a moment then gently laugh.

"Tyler will do it," Ryan says, giving Tyler a shove.

"Let's do it, Emma. Let's get this shit started," he says before chugging the remainder of his beer. He jumps into the water next to me, covering my sunglasses with water drops.

"Dude, don't you know the golden rule?" I ask. "Never splash the glasses."

"Whatever. Race you to the edge! Loser jumps first," he says while taking off toward shore.

I hand my drink, noodle, and glasses to Courtney and do my best to catch up to Tyler. Halfway to the shore, I see that Tyler has already made it and is standing on a large rock just above the water line. The remainder of the swim I take my time, saving my energy for the short hike to the top of the canyon. Reaching shore, I find Tyler staring at me in disbelief.

"Took you long enough," he says, annoyed.

"Whatever," I respond, amused. Courtney was correct, his personality is extremely black and white, hot and cold.

We begin our ascent around the back of the large rock face that will become our jumping-off point. The ground is mainly fine dirt, a few rocks, and other detritus. Our feet are bare, so the walk up the gentle grade is slow until we reach a hefty boulder. Tyler ascends the rock quickly then leans down and offers me a hand. My feet find the proper footing as I take Tyler's hand and launch myself up onto the rock. Without a scratch, Tyler and I stand at the top of the precipice and enjoy the panoramic view. We can hear the cat-calls and dares beginning to rise from the boaters below us.

I take a few deep breaths and allow the slight breeze to cool the remaining water droplets clinging to my skin. The resulting goosebumps disappear quickly under the bright, heavy rays of the sun. Without thought, my hand strokes the turquoise stone hanging gently at the base of my neck, searching for calm and confidence.

"Ladies first," Tyler says with a smirk.

"We both know you're not a gentlemen. I think you are just too chicken to jump first," I challenge.

"I did win the race to the shore, and a bet is a bet," he responds calmly.

"Whatever." I turn toward the water and evaluate my jump. Jumping from a boulder into the lake is no problem, but riding in a boat without a life vest is inconceivable. I'm a walking contradiction with no fudge to give at this point in life. The volume of the whistles and taunts below increases with every passing second. The peanut gallery does not have any patience for jumpers.

"Stay to your right from this spot," Tyler points

below. "There is a boulder under the water to your left, so if you jump slightly right, you should be good to go."

I take in the crowds below, hooting and hollering for us to jump. Several cash offers have been made for me to remove my swim top, but that's not really my thing.

I look to Tyler. "On five," I say. "One... two... three... four... five."

I take two long strides and jump from the edge, launching myself toward the right side of my perch. This is going to hurt, so I place one arm over my boobs to prevent the loss of my top and pinch my nostrils together with my other hand.

Pointing my toes down, I feel the water crash around me, my head pounded from each direction by the rushing water. Releasing my arms from their positions, I kick and stroke myself to the surface. My head breaches the water's surface, and I hear the roar of the raucous boaters around me. I smile because I did it. Glancing upward, I see Tyler wave to me. I wave in return and swim to the side, awaiting his jump.

Tyler makes his jump with a little less fanfare. We high-five each other and swim back toward

Ryan's and Courtney's boat. I smile to myself, hoping this enjoyable morning is indicative of what's to come.

three

CLIMBING THE LADDER BACK ONTO THE rear swim deck of the boat, I grab a towel, my sunglasses, and another cold Mango. My legs hang off the deck into the water as I soak in the sun.

"Nice jump, Em," Courtney calls from the side of the boat where she is still floating with her noodle.

I laugh because it was fun. "Yeah, not bad. I managed to keep my top from floating away too. So that's a win-win if I've ever seen one," I say.

"I'm sure there are plenty of disappointed guys out there," Courtney smirks at Tyler.

I look around, and there are boats everywhere.

Stereos are blasting tunes. Laughter echoes up the side of the hills. The boat now anchored next to us is occupied by three guys. I check them out covertly, my eyes hidden behind the dark tint of my sunglasses, and they are not bad looking- a few tattoos, a bad haircut- but nothing too disturbing. "Hey, what's Ryan doing over on that boat?" I nod toward the other boat where Ryan is standing on the rear swim step.

"Oh, those are some guys Ryan and Tyler know from work, I guess. I've met them a few times out here. Although, I should clarify, I know the boat owner, Brandon, and I have been introduced to the other two, but I don't really know them."

Courtney, Tyler, and I spend the next hour or so chatting about ridiculous things, reminiscing about our antics from high school and college. Tyler tells us some funny stories about his job and his crew. Like that time he was measuring a house for an addition, and he happened upon the wife going to the bathroom. Apparently, the master bath had huge open windows that faced the rear of the property, so there were no privacy shutters or curtains. The wife started screaming, and Tyler ran back to his truck in a panic. He double-checked the address on his paperwork and saw everything was correct, so he called the homeowner to inquire, as the property was supposed to be empty. The husband had assumed the wife would be at the club or some school function and never told her that Tyler would be by to measure. We laugh hysterically as he recalls knocking on the door and explaining himself.

Ryan has boarded our boat once again, followed by Courtney, where they sit quietly under the shade provided by the bimini. They appear deep in conversation, so I turn back to Tyler.

"Tell me more stories! I love this. I work in pharmaceutical sales, and let me tell you, I have no good stories that don't involve bodily functions or nerdy doctor-speak," I pronounce.

Tyler begins a telling me a story about a broken water main when Courtney interrupts.

"Guys, I'm sorry. I'm really not feeling well, and I think it's best if I go back to the trailer and relax," she says quietly.

"Oh no, Court. Is everything ok? Are you sure you don't just need a few minutes to rally instead?"

"I'm sure, Em," she says, looking at Ryan then turning back to me.

"It's not common knowledge, but I'm pregnant."

She smiles gently.

I want to scream and cry, I'm so happy for her, but something is off about her demeanor.

"I know you, Court, what's going on? Is everything ok with the baby?"

"Yes, the baby is good. I'm still very early in the pregnancy, and my blood sugar is a concern, but otherwise I'm healthy. Baby is healthy," she says, holding Ryan's hand between hers.

"I'm so glad. How exciting for you guys! You must be over the moon. I bet your mom went bananas when you told her the news."

She laughs gently, "Yeah, Mom is excited for her first grandchild." I see Courtney's face turn pale, then she lifts her hand to her mouth in horror. A few moments pass and the color returns to her face.

"I've had awful morning sickness. The doctors have asked me to be extremely careful until we determine if my blood sugar is holding steady. I'm sorry to ruin the day for you."

"Do not apologize. We can do this anytime. What's important is you take care of yourself."

Tyler had apparently swum over to the other boat and is now returning. "Brandon said you and I can hitch a ride with his crew if we want to stay out on the lake. What do you say?" he asks me.

I look at Courtney for guidance.

"You should totally go with them. I'm fine. Ryan will be with me, and I'm sure it's just morning sickness. The sun and the heat have taken their toll as well."

"Are you sure? I really don't mind going back to the trailer with you."

"I'm positive. Somebody should have a good time even if it isn't me. Go with them. Brandon takes good care of his boat, and Tyler will keep an eye on you, won't you, Tyler?" she says, glaring at Tyler.

"Of course I'll keep an eye on her," he says, never moving his eyes from Courtney's. "It's settled then. Grab your stuff and we'll get situated on Brandon's boat," he says, gesturing with his hand to the next boat.

While I'm collecting my things, the two boats tie themselves together to ease the transfer of our belongings. Brandon gives me a strange look when I hand him my life vest and tote bag. "I like my own personal life vest. So sue me," I tell him with a large amount of annoyance. He retreats quickly and stows my items in the side panel behind the driver's seat.

"Come here and give me a hug," I say, wrapping my arms around my dear friend. Courtney looks sad and ill but puts on her best fake smile for me.

"Have fun with the guys, and don't do anything I wouldn't do," she laughs. I'm staring directly in her sunglass-covered eyes with a look that says, *Tell me what's going on.* She responds quietly, "I'm good, really, I am."

"All right, I'll see you tonight. Dinner at 8?"

"Yes, dinner at 8, if you aren't praying to the porcelain gods." She laughs and nudges me toward the next boat. I climb over the rear of the boat and step from one swim deck to the other. The guys do boat stuff, unhooking ropes and buoys, while I get familiar with the new boat. Brandon's boat is huge. And when I say huge, I mean I could lay on the bow of the boat with outstretched arms and legs and not touch tips. It even has headphones hanging next to several of the seats. The front of the boat is completely enclosed and looks like a spork with a missing middle tine. The compartment covering the engine has two vents on top which is new to me, and there are enormous exhaust pipes protruding out the rear. I may not know much about engines, but I know the bigger the pipe, the bigger the motor, or something to that effect. And the bigger the motor, the more power or speed the vehicle possesses. I've never been on a boat as large as this, but I have seen them here at the lake, of course. When I made the decision to stay out on the lake, I didn't consider this boat in my evaluation. Courtney would never allow me to hang out on a boat that is unsafe, so I temper my nerves for the time being.

The guys push Ryan and Courtney away, and their boat idles slowly toward the entrance to the cove. My heart burns from deep in my chest as I wonder if Courtney is telling me all there is to know. I hear the rustle of ice behind me where Tyler is digging through the cooler.

"What's up with Ryan and Courtney?" I ask him without looking his way.

"I don't know what you mean?" he says quickly. "They are great! Work is going well for Ryan."

At this point there isn't anything I can do, so I accept Tyler's response for the time being. Maybe Ryan doesn't confide in Tyler the way Courtney does with me, so he may be oblivious to any problems. But I'll be sure and bring it up with Courtney again this evening. Tyler hands me a cold Mango, and I promptly dismiss it with a hand wave. "Thanks, but my tumbler is over there." I point to my disco ball tumbler sitting in the cup holder to my left.

Tyler laughs, shaking his head back and forth. "Women and their damn cups and coozies," he says, while promptly filling my tumbler with the refreshing drink.

"Cheers!" he says, handing me the tumbler. We promptly clink our drinks together.

Brandon and his two buddies climb back into the boat from the water.

"Hey, Emma, this is Owen and J." Brandon gestures to the guys behind him.

"Hi," I manage to say after checking out Owen's large biceps and the tattoos that cover J's entire body. Owen is a nice looking guy with short trimmed hair and a dark tan and fit body. J is a bit rougher looking. His straight black hair is trimmed into a mohawk that is fastened into a pony tail. Every visible inch of skin is covered in black and grey tattoos less his feet and palms.

"Hey, Emma. How are you?" Owen asks politely. J nods a silent hello in my direction.

"I'm good. Thanks for letting me tag along. I wasn't really thinking when I agreed to hang out with you guys. I'm so going to cramp your style, considering I'm the only girl on board." Seriously what was I thinking? I should have gone with Courtney back to the trailer and enjoyed a chill afternoon with her. We don't hang out together as often since her wedding, and my job has become so crazy. But there's no turning back now, so I have to make the best of my decision and try to have fun.

"No worries. The more the merrier," Owen responds. The guys all raise their drinks together. Slowly realizing what is going on, I raise my disco ball to the group, and we clink cheers once again.

I watch each of them chug their beer cans empty then reach for a fresh brew. All four guys have really nice bodies. Brandon has the most stunning face I have ever seen and an extremely fit body with a few random tattoos scattered across his back. Tyler has a very large, well-developed chest. And Owen is tremendously fit, but his arms are large. Like make-way-for-the-gun-show size arms.

"How do you guys know each other?" I ask, looking at Tyler and Brandon.

Brandon answers for the group, "Owen and I are friends from way back, Tyler and I do a little work together, and J is my employee."

The volume of the crowd in the cove begins to

increase. Chanting and whistling echo off the sloping canyon walls that surround us. I turn to look for the source and see a group of girls have climbed to the top of the jumping rock. The girls are probably in their early twenties, celebrating that their classes are finally over, possibly with graduation on the horizon. I've been up there myself making poor choices, but it was certainly a lot of fun.

A girl in a cherry red bikini reaches behind her and pulls the tie that holds her swim top together, releasing her breasts for the public to admire. She has some seriously fine boobs as far as I can tell from down here. She waves the bikini top over her head like a flag, signaling her impending jump. The other two girls follow in unison then jump in choreographed perfection.

The occupants of the boats surrounding us laugh, cheer, and chug with an easy comfort. *Relax, Emma. Enjoy the beautiful day and stop worrying about things over which you have no control.*

The guys and I get in the water and swim toward the boat next to us where a group of men and women similar to us are relaxing and laughing. Apparently, Brandon knows these people as well, and makes quick work of introducing Owen, Tyler,

J, and me to everyone. I'm horrible at remembering names, so I don't even bother to try. Easy banter is tossed among the group. I end up floating next to the other two girls who treat me kindly. We discuss trivial things like the latest Amazon Prime series we have binge-watched or what to think of the latest trend of colored locks of hair. There is full agreement among us that colored hair clumps are better left to tweens and teens, unless it suits your personal style, which isn't the case for any of us. Who knew we could be so old in our mid-twenties?

Tyler floats over and joins our little group. He has an easy-going manner about him and has the full attention of all the girls within moments. I still think it's odd that I don't remember Tyler from Courtney's wedding. I know it must be because I was too busy fawning over my date. What else from Courtney's wedding did I miss because I was so wrapped up in taking care of my date? Those familiar feelings of frustration begin to bubble deep in my gut. How could I not see that the few guys I have dated weren't really into me? It's not like they ignore me or treat me poorly – they just never seem to put me ahead of their friends. In my mind, I see myself as a dart board, an easy target, perhaps, and I just happen to be willing to ignore certain signals in favor of an easy relationship. Courtney likes to remind me that I'm almost never without a boyfriend, which is funny considering she used to be the same way. Looking back, I see that Courtney was different, though; she had all kinds of guys chasing her. She likes to remind me that is how she found Ryan – she sifted through all the weeds until she found her tree, her permanent place to plant her roots where they would firmly grow and flourish.

Ugh, why do I do this to myself? Shaking my head slightly to knock these thoughts from my mind, I focus on the topic among the group. Tyler is telling the girls a story about another lake trip during one of the big holiday weekends where the atmosphere was crazy. I hear him saying things like pasties, thongs, and people passed out, but I'm not wholly paying attention. I'm enjoying the caress of the water against my skin and the gentle breeze that passes over the top of the water.

"Tyler and Emma, let's get going," Brandon shouts as he waves us back to the boat. "We are going to hit up The Dry Heat for some drinks."

"See you over there," one of the girls says to Tyler, and then they swim toward their boat.

"Are they going with us?" I ask Tyler.

"Yeah, they will meet us up there at some point," he says as he climbs aboard the rear deck of the boat. He holds out his hand for me as I navigate the tiny ladder that rests on the back of the boat. Once inside, we secure our belongings, put trash away, and prepare for our departure.

I quietly grab my life vest and towel and take a seat along the rear bench of the vessel. The moment Brandon turns the key and the engine roars to life, I slip my arms through the vest as discreetly as possible and secure the two top buckles. Wrapping the towel around my damp body, I try to hide the life vest as much as I can.

Owen sits down next to me as the boat eases away from the group and idles toward the mouth of the cove. J is sitting in the far corner of the bench next to Owen.

"What's with the life vest?" Owen asks me. I can't see his eyes behind his sunglasses, so I'm not sure what to make of his question. Is he joking or genuinely asking?

"I just need it," I say quietly.

"No big deal. Just wondering if you need it for help swimming or something. I'll keep a closer eye on you if you aren't the best swimmer," he states. Apparently he didn't see me jump from the rock earlier and swim unassisted back to the boat.

"I'm an excellent swimmer. You don't need to worry about me," I say.

"I worry about everyone when we are out here on the lake. People do stupid things when alcohol and limited clothing are involved," he says matter-of-factly.

Who is this guy? A nice-looking man with a conscience and concern for his friends – unheard of here on the lake. Don't get me wrong, there are plenty of nice guys out here, but typically they forget their manners and allow their dicks to dictate their actions. At least, that's what my limited experience has taught me.

Brandon signals to us with a wave of his hand as the engine propels the boat forward very quickly. My heart races as the force of the boat pins my body to the seat. What have I done? This boat is nothing like Courtney's and Ryan's. I notice that Brandon and Tyler have donned the headphones and appear to be talking to each other. My fingers grasp the metal hand grip next to my seat, my knuckles turning white while the burn of the searing hot metal against my skin does nothing to distract me from the fear growing in my mind.

The boat feels like it coasts along the top of the water, sometimes lifting from the water and then settling back down, my body left floating slightly off the seat. My eyes watch my knuckles turn white as I cling to the hand grip with every bit of strength I can summon. Closing my eyes, I concentrate on regulating my breathing and clearing my mind.

I'm startled by the heavy weight of another body settling next to me. Owen has pushed his body against mine, wedging me neatly into the corner of the bench seat. My face turns from full frown to part frown, part smile. He smiles down at me and pats my leg gently as if signaling his understanding of my fear.

Managing to lift my gaze to the water surrounding us, I notice that we are passing boats on the right and left with little effort. The thunder of the air slapping against my ears becomes my focus until I notice we have slowed slightly. Looking ahead, I see The Dry Heat Marina on the horizon. The thudding of my heart against the walls of my chest eases as the boat smoothly slows to an idle, settling deeper into the water.

"Are you ok?" Owen asks honestly.

"Not really, but I think I'll live. What the hell kind of boat is this and how fast were we going?" The questions exit my mouth with no break in between. "Why does it feel like it's not even in the water when we are going that fast?"

Brandon and Tyler chuckle. "It's an offshore-style boat made to travel at extremely high speeds," Owen responds to my question as he gently scoots away from me on the bench. I feel a chill on my leg and look down to see a slick of perspiration where the skin of Owen's thigh was touching mine. The marina docks come into view as Brandon navigates the boat into the small slip with ease.

"We were going 100 if you really want to know," Brandon boasts.

"100 what?" I ask, slightly confused. Is he talking nautical things like knots, and if so what the heck does that mean?

"100 miles per hour. And we could have gone faster, but I didn't want to scare you too much," he chuckles.

Every fiber of my body is overcome with dread when I realize that I still need to get back in this boat to return to town.

"Hey, are you all right?" Owen asks. "Your face is white as a ghost. This is an extremely safe boat, so you don't need to worry." His eyes are warm with concern.

"If you say so," I respond without conviction. I focus on my fingers gliding across my precious turquoise, envisioning calm, willing away my negative attitude.

"Let's go get a Big Stick and some lunch, and I think you will feel better," he says.

"What is a Big Stick?" I'm both curious and horrified at the thought of what a Big Stick could be.

"It's a cocktail served in a tall, thin glass, kind of like those old-school popsicles. Tastes just like one as well."

I hesitate to respond while shedding my life vest. Removing my tote bag from the compartment where it has been stowed, I slip on a sarong and my flip flops for the walk to the saloon.

"Sounds great!" comes out of my mouth, louder than planned. The guys all chuckle at my outburst.

Brandon, Tyler, J, and Owen make quick work of securing the boat to the dock with rope and buoys. It's amazing how Brandon was able to maneuver this large boat into a tiny little boat slip. I try to convince myself that I shouldn't be so worried. It seems like this vessel is well cared for and Brandon knows what he is doing. I wonder when I became such a worry-wart – man, I'm annoying. Note to self to work on my attitude. Thousands of people boat and have fun every weekend with no problems, no drownings.

"Somebody is ready to get her drink on," Tyler says, offering me his hand. I step onto the towel-covered seat and allow Tyler's hand to propel me effortlessly onto the dock. The reflection of the sun off the dock burns into my shins as we quickly walk toward the air conditioned comfort of the saloon. I try to erase my worries from their prominence in my mind, but I fail to make purchase. A drop of perspiration slides down the side of my neck as I walk into the marina bar. The cold air settles onto my skin leaving goosebumps in its path.

four

INSIDE THE SALOON, WE SECURE A LARGE HIGH-top table that will seat our whole party. The waitress swiftly appears with cups and a large pitcher of ice water for our table. Brandon orders Big Sticks all around as we gulp down the icy cold water.

"I'm starving," I say. "I haven't done anything physical today, but I feel like I ran a marathon. I forgot how taxing the sun can be on your appetite." The guys chuckle collectively.

Television screens are mounted on either side of the room. Auto racing, hockey, and basketball seem to be the sports of the moment. I watch the cars on the screen speed swiftly around the oval-shaped track. Why do the cars always seem to go left? The front of the building is mostly glass which faces the water and marina. A wall-length bar flanks the windows, giving patrons sitting at the traditional bar a beautiful view of the lake. The saloon is rectangular-shaped with tan walls and typical restaurant-style vinyl booths. A dozen hi- top tables run down the middle of the room in varying configurations. The rear of the room houses a dart board, a pool table, and two video games. A burst of voices erupts from the door. Looking over my shoulder, I see the crew from the cove. Hellos are said again as everyone settles into their seats. Tyler is on my left and the girls are on my right. Owen, Brandon, and J are sitting across from me chatting amongst themselves.

The waitress appears with our drinks, and wow, the guys weren't kidding when they said this drink is big. It reminds me of the huge themed drinks you purchase in Vegas. The Eiffel Tower and the Statue of Liberty are hiding in my kitchen somewhere, hoping to be filled once again.

The Big Stick is a cylinder-shaped glass about twelve inches tall, filled with red and orange slushy goodness. We each take a long sip through the bendy straw protruding from the top, allowing the icy-cold sweet and sour liquid to chill our throats.

"That is tasty!" I proclaim to the table.

Everyone chuckles and begins telling tales of the aftermath of Big Sticks at the lake. They are typical stories, similar to those I hear from Courtney and Ryan. For example, somebody passing out and getting a random sunburn, or getting "Van Goghed" while you are sleeping. You know, when somebody draws a fake mustache on your upper lip or a penis on your forehead. Sure, it's juvenile. But it's amazingly funny to watch when the person awakes and has no knowledge of the penis penned prominently across his face.

The waitress delivers a round of shots to the table. Eyeing mine suspiciously, I wonder if this is a good idea. I can handle my drinks, but maybe I should refrain from having anymore alcohol today. Shots are tipped back around me with cheers and high-fives as I contemplate the situation. Brandon is talking animatedly to our tablemates causing me to wonder how much he's had to drink. I'm such a damn worry-wart today but this is important to consider.

"Hey, are you going to drink that?" Tyler asks, nodding to the shot.

"Please, you have it. I can't drink another thing." Tyler tips the shot to me in thanks and downs the liquid in one gulp. We order food and start a friendly game of darts at the back of the room. Owen takes me as his partner, which is comforting considering he seems the most pleasant of the men in the group. Two girls and two guys from the other party round out the three teams. We drink in comfortable silence as we await our turn at the board. My stomach is overcome from the smell of burgers and fries cooking, mixed with the tropical scent of sunscreen that is no doubt slathered across everyone's skin.

Fortunately, Owen is great at small talk. My estimation is that he's a genuine man, not a player like I had initially guessed. He asks me about my job and gets me chatting with ease. I enjoy the time talking with Owen and start feeling more like myself. It's nice to be with a group of people, and among single men, with no expectation of finding a boyfriend or a date, wondering if anyone likes me, or constantly thinking about whether I like any of these men. Brandon's animated voice in the background gives me pause to reconsider his suitability to captain the boat back to town. Owen's gentle and polite demeanor give me the confidence to breach the subject.

"Do you think Brandon will be too drunk to drive us back?" I ask quietly, watching Owen's face for any type of tell. His face remains creaseless, but he quickly runs his hand through his hair and exhales deeply. The good vibes are not radiating from Owen.

"I gave him a hard time about the shot he took. He promised he was done drinking, and we still have lunch to eat, so he's fine. We aren't leaving for about an hour, so we will be all good. Brandon can get a little crazy, but he won't risk damaging his boat with his stupidity." I glance over my shoulder to see Brandon at the table with a glass of water in his hand, chatting with J.

I contemplate Owen's words carefully and decide to leave the matter for the time being. Our turn arrives as the third pair in the game. Owen does well, garnering one bullseye and two other well-placed darts. All three of my darts land on the outside ring. We take turns until the game has played out. Surprisingly, Owen and I came in second. The losing pair has to buy the next round for the entire group at the table, but I politely decline another drink as does Brandon, much to my relief.

Our food arrives, providing everyone a much needed recharge. The guys are talking sports again. The level of Tyler's voice continues to rise as does the slur in his speech. The Big Stick glass and several other empty cups sit prominently in front of him. Clearly, Tyler has consumed more than his share of alcohol. Thankfully, he takes a large bite of his burger while I observe him, and he appears to have no fresh cocktails in his possession. I excuse myself to the restroom and temporarily escape the raucous laughter. Hearing footsteps behind me, I glance over my shoulder to see Hailey, one of the girls I met earlier out on the lake, heading in my direction. I managed to remember her name while we were sitting at the table chatting, thank goodness. Her steps quicken as she catches up to me at the restroom door.

"Guys are always the ones to get stupid, aren't they?" she asks emphatically with a slight eye roll. I laugh in response, opening the door and stepping into one of the stalls. Tyler and another guy are jeering loudly enough for me to hear them through the bathroom walls.

"So what's the deal with you? Are you with any

of the guys in your boat? Any potential boyfriends?" Hailey prods.

Laughter erupts from my mouth before I can temper it and formulate an appropriate response. "I'm just along for the ride. No boyfriends, no prospects, no men for me," I say, realizing I mean every word I said. For the first time in what feels like forever, I'm not searching for my next boyfriend.

"So you don't mind if I chat up Brandon?" Hailey responds.

"Feel free," I say, meaning it. Hailey is a cute girl with thick blonde hair that is currently braided over one shoulder. She has light brown eyes that sparkle when she smiles, and she would look adorable on the arm of Brandon with his natural good looks. Based on appearances, they seem to be a good match, but what do I know? I can't even choose a good guy for myself.

Hailey continues chatting about Brandon and the new lip gloss she is currently applying. We wash our hands and head back to the group. Owen is waiting at the empty table for Hailey and me.

"Where is everyone?" I ask Owen.

"They are down on the docks. We paid the bill and are heading out to a quieter beach."

The sound of the door slamming and shouting coming from the entrance draws us to the front of the saloon. Brandon and Tyler are arguing with each other. Tyler appears to have trouble standing up straight without leaning on the wall.

"Hey, there she is. Little Emma with the life vest," Tyler slurs in my direction, a smile plastered on his face.

"That's enough," Brandon implores.

"What's your deal, bro?" Tyler shouts at Brandon. "I'm just having a good time. Can't I have a good time with Life Vest Emma?" he says while trying to walk in my direction.

"Don't be an ass," Owen says with a glare at Tyler.

"What's your problem, dude. You want Life Vest Emma for yourself? I'm cool with that. Or we can share."

"I called you a taxi, bro. It will be here in 10 minutes, so chill out until the car arrives, alright?" Brandon says while grasping Tyler's arm in an attempt to guide him outside.

Tyler starts swearing and arguing with Brandon, and before I realize what's happening, Tyler attempts to throw a punch at Brandon but misses completely and finds himself careening in my direction. He trips over his own foot, causing his body to slam into mine, knocking me off my feet, and both of us fall to the ground with a head-cracking thud.

The heat of embarrassment flushes my cheeks red as the guys pull Tyler off me. Together, Owen and J carry Tyler outside to wait for his driver to arrive. Brandon and Hailey offer a hand to help me from the floor.

Dusting myself off, I realize this could have been worse. My body parts are intact, and I managed to avoid hitting my head by using my arm to brace against the fall.

"Guys can be total jerks," Hailey says, as she bends to retrieve my tote bag from the ground.

"What is it with guys and drinking and then getting mean?" I ask, looking directly at Brandon.

"Girls can be just as mean, but I know what you are getting at. Guys always blow up a good time with their fists," Hailey states. Brandon smirks and heads outside.

"Where did the rest of your group go?" I ask.

"They left already to head back to town. Brandon said I could join you guys, so I'm on his boat now."

Owen walks in from the front door and waves

us outside. "Tyler's ride is here. Let's head down to the boat and leave this mess behind. It's only one o'clock. We have plenty of time to resurrect a good day."

The events of the last few minutes seem to have sobered our group, which I gratefully accept as a blessing. J is already at the boat waiting. Owen helps Hailey and me onto the boat and begins removing the lines and buoys from the dock. Brandon jogs down the dock from the saloon with a smile on his face.

"Let's try this again," he laughs. "Tyler can be such a tool sometimes," he says to Owen and J.

Brandon takes his seat behind the controls while J and Owen continue their work. Hailey and I get situated, stowing our flip flops and bags. I quietly settle into my preferred seat along the rear of the boat, while Hailey takes the chair next to the driver. Thankful that Hailey won't be able to see me, I swiftly secure my life vest in place and settle deep into the thickly cushioned seat.

While Brandon starts the boat and reverses out of the boat slip with the ease of a professional, Owen swings the bow of the boat away from the dock and jumps aboard. The pounding in my chest increases as we get further from the marina. My hand gently shakes at my side as I try to calm my breathing. I know I'm being stupid but I can't worry about that right now. Memories of the past threaten to invade my thoughts. Visions of boat crashes flash across my mind, sweat pools at the back of my neck before it trails down my back disappearing into my life vest. Feelings of loss attempt to invade my thoughts, but I manage to push them aside.

Owen plops down next to me and gives my thigh a gentle pat. Brandon again gives the "go" hand signal before the boat launches forward. The comfort of Owen's leg scooting next to mine calms my otherwise erratic breathing. I focus on the back of the seat in front of me and hope for the best. My face is battered by loose strands of hair as the wind destroys my top knot. I welcome the distraction.

Several minutes pass before I feel the boat slow to a comfortable pace. When your boat goes 100 miles per hour, you navigate from beach to beach very quickly. Wiping the hair from my face and lifting my eyes, I see we have arrived at our next destination. It's a small cove with a thick beach surrounded by reeds and gently rolling hills covered in low desert shrubs. Our beach is located in a state park that is monitored by boat and accessible by four-wheel drive from a road somewhere in the middle of the desert. Half a dozen picnic tables dot the length of the beach, and an outhouse is visible on the downward side of a hill in the distance. A handful of boats rest on the beach as children are play. The adults appear to be older and calmer than the group we encountered earlier in the day.

Brandon slides the boat onto the sand near the edge of the beach. We gather our things and hop out of the boat. Owen produces chairs for each of us so we can set up a small camp. This is definitely more my speed. I enjoy the sun warming my legs as we chat about work and life. Brandon tells us details about the projects he is hoping to land over the next few months. J isn't much of a talker but he participates in the conversation in short spurts. I learn that Owen works in finance and secures investors for some of Brandon's projects. If I was allowed to look for a boyfriend, I might consider Owen. He's handsome, educated, and well- mannered. Pushing the thought aside, I remind myself this is how I get into trouble.

The afternoon ticks by peacefully. We enjoy a few drinks, the shining sun, good conversation, and the tickle of water on our toes. It has to be close to three o'clock when two boats appear in the distance. Brandon stands and waves his arm at the boats.

"These are a few of my buddies. Looks like another party," he says, a huge grin spreading across his face.

J stands from his chair, joining Brandon to help the other boats onto the sand. There have to be fifteen people on these two boats, which makes this an instant party. Goosebumps spawn across my legs where the breeze has caused the water to spray delicately. Disappointment clouds my mind for a minute, but I shake it off. The entire day has been a dramatic climb and fall of emotions for me. One minute I'm doing great, having a good time; the next, I'm dreading being social or questioning my decision to remain on the lake while Courtney returned to the comfort of the trailer.

This has never been me. I'm always up for a good time and can talk to most people with ease; but today, I feel out of sorts. The nagging feeling in the back of my mind continues to lurk. Waiting for something bad to happen is not how I approach life, generally speaking. But for some reason, I'm nothing but fear today. Plastering a fake smile on my face, I decide to work myself out of the dumps and join the rest of the group.

Hailey has already taken her place near Brandon, so I head toward Owen where he is chatting with three girls from the other boats. He seems extremely confident. Courtney didn't give me the inside scoop on Owen, but I feel like he has his pick of willing women in his life. Gratefully, Owen sees me approaching, and with a small wave of his hand, manages to calm my nerves. He makes introductions, but once again, I don't bother to listen to the names because it will take me days to remember each of them.

There is an easy chemistry in our little group, and as the minutes pass, the gloomy cloud over my mood subsides, allowing me to enjoy the beach once again. The girls want to go for a swim, but I politely decline; at this point, I have had enough swimming for the day.

"Hey, grab your shoes and we'll take a short hike back into the canyon," Owen suggests to me.

"Hike? As in walk among bugs and snakes?" I sound petulant.

"Bugs are everywhere, but the sun is out, so the snakes should be under cover and won't bother us," he says, like they are merely flies on the window.

"I hate snakes. Seriously. I would rather ride in Brandon's boat without my life vest than go anywhere near snakes."

"You'll be fine. I'm not keen on snakes either, but it's a nice walk along the base of the hill. There is a worn footpath, so we won't be tramping on unspoiled land."

"I don't know," I utter. But realizing I sound like a big baby, I say determinedly, "Let's do it!" before I can change my mind.

Owen grabs my flip flops from the boat and bottles of water for each of us. We leave the group without a word, as they are mesmerized by the girls now lounging on the lily pad, a giant floating piece of foam. I notice Brandon has a beer, and I begin to wonder if he has started drinking again, if this is just one beer or the start of several. Making a mental note to discuss this with Owen when we return from our hike, I turn and head toward the hills.

"Let's go!" Owen shouts from up ahead.

"I'm coming!" Increasing my pace, I quickly catch up to Owen as he finds the footpath in the middle of the beach. There is a small sand hill that separates the beach from the canyon. With little work, we breach the top of the hill and head down into the pristine desert.

"This is the best part of the desert, in my opinion. You get the beauty of the desert, but the proximity to the lake means there is a greater abundance of reeds and wildflowers." Owen talks as though he's a tour guide, pointing out different varieties of cactus.

"Watch out for this cholla. They are known to reach out and grab you, leaving needles as a parting gift," he chuckles, pointing to this prickly bush near the edge of the trail. I carefully walk around it, keeping as much distance as possible.

Owen is physically attractive with light brown hair and dark brown eyes set perfectly over a proportionate nose. He has a strong, but not too large chin and a five-o'clock-shadow that would cause any woman to swoon. A handful of small tattoos are scattered across his deeply tanned and fit body. His biceps are extremely well-developed, but he isn't one of those scary huge guys that are nothing but muscle. My first impression of him was that he would be like a lot of the guys out here: confident, cocky, and an asshole. This wouldn't be the first or last time my impression of a guy proved wrong.

"Emma. Are you there?" Owen asks while stepping closer to me. I didn't realize he was calling my name.

"Sorry, just enjoying the scenery and I zoned out," I say. He smiles in response.

"Shh. Do you hear that?" He puts his hands out indicating for me not to move. In the distance, I hear it. Owen begins walking slowly as we near the crest of another small hill. Stopping quickly, he glances over his shoulder at me with a large smile. I take a few steps forward so I'm standing next to him when I see it.

A desert burro is walking idly down toward the beach about a hundred yards from our perch. Movement near the water catches my eye, and I see two more burros drinking from the edge of the lake. The animals are prominent in this part of the desert due to the lake proximity.

"They are so cute!" I exclaim. Owen chuckles in response.

"What is it with girls and animals? 'Animals are so cute!'" He mimics my voice and makes an odd gesture with his hands.

"What is that arm flailing you're doing? Is that supposed to be your best impression of a girl?" I joke, laughing when he drops his arms to his sides.

"Yeah, I was never much of an actor." He smiles, returning his gaze to the burros.

"Let's keep going for a bit then turn around," he suggests.

"Sounds good to me." The sun has started to lower in the sky, but the heat in the air remains, generating trails of sweat from the back of my neck and between my boobs.

"I'm sure I smell great," I mutter to myself.

"You smell fine," Owens says over his shoulder.

"I wasn't talking to you," I say in jest, then change the subject. "So, you were saying you are in finance or investments? That must be cool. I wouldn't have pegged you for a paper-pusher."

"I'm sort of in both, I guess. I find investors and group them together based on the finance needs of my clients. Mostly, I do construction and investment property financing, which has its own set of quirks and problems like most businesses, but I enjoy it. Didn't anyone ever tell you not to judge a book by its cover?" he smirks.

"Touché," I say as we reach the top of another small hill. Owen abruptly stops, causing me to run into his back. "What's going on?" I ask, trying to peer around him.

"Look ahead to the west, midway up the canyon where there is a natural shelf."

My eyes travel across the canyon searching for movement, but I fail to see anything. "What is it?" I ask quietly.

"There," he says quickly, pointing directly ahead. The lithe body of a coyote appears from the other side of a boulder, jogging swiftly away from our position. The sun sparkles against the animal's beautiful coat of silver, brown, and gold.

"It's stunning. Who knew desert coyotes could be so beautiful?" I ask.

"Pretty cool," Owen responds as we watch the coyote disappear deep into the canyon. "This might be a good point to turn back. We've been gone almost an hour, and by the time we reach the beach, it will be time to pack up and head back to town."

"This was a great idea," I say. "Thanks for suggesting it. I wasn't really feeling that party vibe back there. I'm not sure what's up with my mood today, but this was a welcome distraction. So, thanks," I say, looking up, trying to see beneath his sunglasses.

"My pleasure. I usually end up hiking by myself, so the company is appreciated," he says. Turning around in place, I'm now the unwilling lead as we weave our way back along the trail. I'm not shy about my body, but the realization that Owen is walking behind me while I'm wearing nothing but a bikini causes the sun-kissed blush on my cheeks to sharpen red.

"Why don't you let me be in front so I can check for snakes and bugs? I wouldn't want you to be the first person the critters encounter."

"Gladly," I respond without hesitation. Stopping on the trail, I move to the side so Owen can pass me. The trail is only wide enough to walk single-file, making it impossible for Owen to pass without touching me.

"Don't worry, I don't bite," he says, gently holding my shoulders as he scoots along my body. His chest brushes against my boobs, causing my body to respond inappropriately. *Not here, please, not here*, I tell my hypersensitive breasts. Under the guise of adjusting my swim suit, I attempt to pull the top away from my pointed nipples.

The return hike is uneventful as we set a steady pace back to the beach. Owen crests the hill in front of us that leads down to the beach then stops sharply. I'm lost in thought as I walk around him, heading down to the shore and the comfort of the sand and water. I definitely need a dip in the water. My bathing suit is soaked in sweat, and I think a trail of perspiration has traveled down between my cheeks. Looking over my shoulder I see Brandon perched at the same spot on the hill, scanning the beach.

Returning my gaze forward, I notice only two boats remain. The edge of the beach where the reed growth begins is empty, not a single boat is waiting in the water next to our beach chairs. Owen's shadow appears before he stops next to me. We both stare at the empty beach with curiosity.

"They probably went for a boat ride and will be back soon. Don't worry," Owens says, then continues toward the shore where our abandoned chairs remain. Kicking off my flip flops, I enter the water in search of relief from the heat and the layer of dust that has become plastered to my body. Floating gently, I allow myself to enjoy the cradle of water that has surrounded me and the warmth of the day's final rays of sun on my face. The trickle and splash of water alerts me to Owen's presence.

"I checked my phone and there are no bars out here. Brandon can be a dick, but I'm sure he will be back soon. He's never left me behind on past trips."

"Are you trying to convince me or yourself?" I ask him pointedly.

"Both, I think," he answers quietly.

Owen doesn't strike me as the dramatic type, which only further raises the concerns churning through my brain. Concerns which are proving difficult to discredit.

We float in silence, watching boats travel by the small inlet where our beach is located, hoping that one will be Brandon.

The crowd on the beach begins to pack up their things onto the remaining two boats. I watch with curiosity as Owen exits the water and walks down the beach toward them. After a brief conversation, I see the boat occupants hand a bag to Owen, who gently places it on the beach.

With a turn of the ignition, the boat's engine roars to life, echoing along the hills as goosebumps appear along my arms. The hair on the back of my neck tingles causing a shiver to roll through my body, unease settling over me like black coffee on an empty stomach. I watch as Owen pushes the boat away from the beach and into the open water. The captain gives a hearty wave as the boat slowly disappears from view.

Exiting the water, I grab my flip flops and walk the short distance to where Owen has settled on a picnic bench. My emotions turn over and over, from fear to calm, reality to denial.

As though he senses the whirlwind of emotion traveling through my mind, Owen tries to calm my nerves. "Don't worry, Emma. That group of people in the last boat said Brandon left just a few minutes before we returned. They were kind enough to offer us a ride, but I declined. Riding in a boat with strangers who may have had too much to drink isn't my idea of fun, I hope you don't mind. Plus I think both of the boats were over the recommended passenger weight. They gave me a bag with some water, a few beers, and half a bag of chips to pass the time until Brandon returns," he says with a genuine smile.

"You're right. They'll be back soon," I say. Retreating deep into my mind, I take a seat at the table facing the lake which has become quiet. Only the lap of water against the shore breaks the silence.

The pop and fizz of a can opening startles me back into reality.

"May as well make the best of an annoying situation," Owen says, holding out an open can of beer for me. I take it from his hand, willing a smile to appear on my face. "If that isn't the most depressing smile I've ever seen," he chuckles.

"Sorry, I'm trying not to be a downer. I'm sure Brandon will be back soon or the park ranger will come. It's not like we are stranded in the middle of the desert without the possibility of someone finding us," I say.

"All we can do right now is make the best of the situation," he says honestly, as he pops open a beer for himself. "Tell me more about yourself."

five

THE SUN BREACHES THE PEAK OF THE mountains to the west, a pie-shaped slice now missing from its outline. Owen and I pass the time drinking beer and chatting about everything and nothing. His calm demeanor eases my fears. Or maybe it's the beer. Either way, I relax into the comfortable conversation.

After telling stories about our work, the good and the bad, our conversation turns more personal.

"Where is your boyfriend this weekend?" Owens prods as he opens another beer. I was shocked to find ten cans of beer in the bag given to us by the other boaters. At least something good has happened today.

"I don't have a boyfriend," I say, hoping he doesn't pry into my disaster of a dating life.

"Why not? You're a good-looking girl, and you seem relatively easy going, other than a few random quirks I've noticed today. Not looking or not interested?" he inquires.

"Thanks for that *you're nice but weird* compliment," I chuckle.

Sensing I'm not going to get away from this conversation, I decide to be brutally honest so we can move forward from the topic of my life. "I had a boyfriend, but we recently parted ways," I say, looking blankly at Owen.

"What happened?"

"Don't know. I guess we got tired of each other. You know how it goes—after you get comfortable with someone, you find out the truth."

"What do you mean 'the truth'? Did he have another girl on the side? Was he secretly cheating on you with his PlayBOX gaming buddies while denying he even played video games? Did he keep it a secret that he has a strange foot fetish? He had a bunch of women's shoes hidden deep in his closet, didn't he?" he laughs. It's obvious by our silly demeanors that the beer is definitely getting to both of us.

I laugh out loud. "Yep, he kept stealing my shoes, the really old ones that should have been donated or thrown out. Like, why didn't he want my newer cute shoes? I can't hang with a guy who only wants something old, slightly smelly, and scuffed beyond hope."

"Exactly. You need to find a guy who wants to hoard your cute shoes. Everyone knows that." We both laugh from deep in our bellies.

"I was actually in a bad mood coming out on this little trip. Despite all the difficulties of the day, and our situation, it's turned out to be a nice break from my life. So thanks for that."

"Why do you need a break from your regular life, Emma? You talk fondly of your job and co-workers, and I know you have a few good friends because you are here with Ryan and Courtney. So what would cause you to need a break? How old are you anyway?"

"I'm twenty-five. Geez, how many questions are you going to ask? Don't you ever feel the need to get away from life, from the everyday monotony of going to work and adulting?"

"I don't feel that way, no," he responds, a crease

forming between his eyebrows.

"How is that even possible? Everyone wants a break to be free. To forget about work, or your broken down car, or rent that's due," I say, incredulous. The turquoise around my neck presses delicately into the skin of my neck reminding me to work away the negative thoughts.

"My life is good, so I try to concentrate on the positive. I love my job, I'm fortunate to have understanding and supportive parents, and my sister and I have a great relationship. There's nothing I can do but pay my rent and forge ahead. The cards will fall as they are played, so I may as well accept the hand I've been dealt and make the best of it. You never know when that lonely pair of twos will become a winning a hand."

Considering Owen's statement, I think about how my emotions play a significant role in guiding my life. How do I allow myself to stick my head in the sand and hide from everything in front of me? My finger works a crevice along the length of the greenish-blue stone with a rhythmic precision.

"Mister Positive Thinker, over here," I respond with a smirk.

"What can I say, it's just who I am."

My mind takes a sudden turn into pity mode. I'm don't view myself as a negative person, but everything Owen said resonates into my life as an example of who I am not. When did my view of life become so skewed? Since I broke up with Drew my mind has been all over the place. Is it because I'm unsettled at the thought of being alone? Even with Drew, I felt lonely. I'm worth more than that. Being alone is not the same as being lonely. I've put myself into this tiny little box that I view as perfect, and when my life falls outside the box I become negative, question my choices. I never want to be in that box again – life is better when I choose my happiness over a man's. The time has come for me to acknowledge my weakness and move on. My person is out there somewhere, I may as well enjoy trying to find him. Like Courtney said, no boyfriends, only one-night stands.

"What's going on in that pretty little head over there?" Owen says with a gentle tap on my shoulder.

Tears of my alcohol-induced pity party threaten to fall from my eyes. Blinking quickly, I will them away for now. "Thinking," I say respond flatly.

"Thinking about what?"

I feel a shudder pulsate through my body as

Owen continues to prod, and I realize this conversation is not going to disappear.

"You have an amazing outlook on life. It makes me sad to think I have allowed my attitude to become so skewed, how I view life in a negative light instead of a positive one. I don't want to worry about all this nonsense. I've always been a hard worker. I can accept even the worst news, get angry, and then forge ahead with a new plan. But in doing so, I've become negative myself. I willingly fall head over heels for guys who don't treat me badly, but they don't treat me with respect either. Courtney likes to remind me that I have been this way with guys since high school. I always fall madly over someone who shows a small amount of interest in me. I adore them, care for them, and treat them exactly how I want to be treated. But in return I have never received the same consideration. I want to be cherished. I want a man to fall over himself for me, as I will do for him. I'm beginning to think the idea is merely a fairytale. A story never to be told by me. I want to hope. I want the old me back, the one not jaded by a string of bad relationships."

"It seems to me you're on your way to finding your fairytale."

"Really?" I say with sarcasm dripping from my lips. "I can feel sand in my ass, the sweat from today is caked to my hairline, and I'm stranded in the middle of the desert with some beer, a bag of half-eaten chips, an outhouse, and a guy I just met today. Sounds like a perfect fairytale to me," I cackle.

"Sometimes we need to stop looking for things and let them happen organically. A situation that may not be ideal could lead to something important. A new job opportunity, a stranger becoming a valued friend, or valuable lessons learned. The fact that you recognize your faults and want to change them is the hardest part of the story. Keep building the foundation for your story and before long your fairytale will appear."

"Are you secretly a motivational speaker? An up-and-coming Dr. Phil wannabe? You're one big contradiction," I say.

"A contradiction? I don't have a clue what you mean. Enlighten me, please," he laughs.

"On the outside, you're attractive. You clearly take care of your body and confidence oozes from your pores. That should make you a narcissistic asshole who uses women for his own physical gratification and then moves on, leaving a trail of destruction in his path. All the guys out there who look like you are douche bags; it's that simple. But you aren't like them at all. You watch over your friends with care and make sure everyone around you is comfortable. My first impression of you was wrong. And for that, I apologize."

"No apology necessary. We all come from different places in the world, suffer different situations that shape of our views, both good and bad," he says honestly. "What I want to know is, what happened to you that made you so cynical? Who put you down so far you can't raise your head in pride?"

"I don't understand," I question with a shake of my head. "Nothing happened to me. I'm the same person I've always been. I'm that person in the middle. The girl who isn't gorgeous or ugly, smart or stupid, shy or outgoing, confident or not. I'm the girl nobody ever sees because I'm background noise. I'm not like Courtney who can talk to a stranger without apprehension or who has a natural physical beauty. I'm just me," I say with a huff.

When Owen doesn't respond, I discreetly glance in his direction to gauge his response. He's watching the last light of day disappear among the ripples of the water, a stick in his hand carves a line in the sand between his feet. I don't probe him for a response out of my own fear of the truth. My gaze returns to the empty beach in contemplation. My eyes raise to the sky, observing the clouds moving across the horizon. Some of the clouds are thick, like giants balls of snow, while others are shapeless and flat, moving across the sky with little notice. I'm like the latter clouds, observed but never really seen.

"I just don't get it," Owen says after a few minutes of silence between us. "How can a girl as pretty, honest, and real as you not know your worth? You have a beautiful smile, an easy spirit and a kind heart. It's like you were never loved in your life, loved for being you. As humans, don't we all, at the end of the day, want to be loved for simply being real? To be true to ourselves and those we care about? I think you, Emma, are the one who is special. It's those guys you dated who have truly lost when they failed to realize how special you are and never treated you accordingly."

I scoff at his remark. "How would you even know about being average? Nothing about you is average. I guarantee you don't want for love, companionship, or acceptance. This is just a load of sunshine you are blowing up my ass for some reason.

Is it pity, maybe? I don't get you at all." Frustration seeps deep into my body as I digest Owen's extremely accurate evaluation of me.

"You can't take a compliment, can't you?" he asks. I don't respond because I'm angry, yet I don't know why.

"Look, I'm not sure how this conversation went sideways, so I'll tell you something personal about myself. Something I don't really want to admit, but I will for the sake of this conversation," he says. I'm intrigued by Owen's comments. Glancing at his face, I see apprehension crease his forehead and humility in his faint smile.

"This is sort of embarrassing, to be honest," he begins. "I don't have a girlfriend."

"That's it?" I say annoyed. "You probably don't have just one. I'm sure you have several," I say flatly.

"Would you let me finish? I promise there's more."

I wave my hand in the air signaling him to continue.

"I've never dated a girl longer than a month or two. And before you interrupt with a crude comment about sleeping around, let me tell you, I'm really not like that," he says, frustrated. "Sure, I'll be honest. At this point, I've slept with my fair share of women. I won't deny that women turn me on, and I'm happy to participate in an evening of mutual satisfaction. But I've yet to meet that girl who blows my mind, the girl who overtakes my every thought and action. I wonder if something in me is broken because I can't connect with a woman on a deeper level," he says, resignation bound to his words.

His words strike me from deep within. We aren't so different after all. I smile at the realization that this good man next to me suffers a similar fate. Maybe this is all normal. I don't know, but I don't feel as alone as I did this morning when I got into the truck with Courtney and Ryan.

"It appears we might have more in common than I suspected," I say.

"How so?" Owen responds. The sound of the stick digging deeper into the sand betrays his anxiety about the topic.

"We both want to be loved. I allow myself to date guys who are not fully invested in me in hopes they will change, and maybe one day, be my everything, love me fully, empower and support me with every fiber of their being. You live in fear that you will never find a girl who does the same for you.

The only difference between us is that you don't settle for less than you deserve, while I do nothing but settle." A smile relaxes across my lips as I come to terms with my flaw.

Chancing a glance at Owen, I see a smile brightening his face, as well. He looks over at me and we both begin to chuckle. The heaviness that had surrounded us lifts, as does my spirit.

"Quite a pair, aren't we?" Owen laughs. "It's comedic. We both came out to the lake for relaxation and to enjoy ourselves, and we end up analyzing each other," he snickers quietly.

The last rays of the sunset have disappeared, cloaking the lake in darkness. I watch the stars twinkle above like the universe winking at me. A shooting star streaks across the sky then disappears like fireworks on the Fourth of July. For the first time in a long time, I feel content with myself, hopeful even. And I'm wondering if this gentle man sitting next to me is for real.

six

WITH DARKNESS COMES THE realization that Brandon won't be coming to get us. The likelihood a park ranger will pass by our location at this time of night is slim. Deep down I feel like I should be scared, certainly angry or frustrated, at the very least. But I'm consumed by an unnatural calmness. Could it be the three cans of beer I have consumed? Or is it something else? I'm not sure, but at this point, I don't see a reason to question my mood.

"Thankfully the weather is calm and monsoon season is still a few weeks away, because it appears we may be here all night," Brandon states matter-of-factly.

"You were so sure Brandon wouldn't leave you here, so sure he would never leave behind a buddy."

"I was wrong, what do you want me to say? This is a first for me," he says, scratching the side of his head. "There are a million worse places we could be stranded, so I'll gladly take this slice of heaven on Earth," he chuckles to himself.

"What about animals or snakes? Won't they travel down from the hills for water? This camping thing is foreign to me," I say to Owen as I stand then lie down on the sand, stretching out my limbs.

"The burros are no danger to us, and I think if we stay here at the widest section of the beach we may not see any snakes, but I can't make any promises," he states. "I'm not worried about being here all night. Somebody will find us tomorrow and return us to town."

"Always the optimist. How many beers do we have left?" I ask as I sit up.

"Plenty," Owen responds with a huge smile. He pulls two beers and the potato chips from the bag, sits down next to me in the sand, and places everything between us. "May as well continue our little party, don't you think?"

I respond happily, "Cheers! Here's to making the best of a bad situation." We clink our cans together and take a long pull from the now warm liquid. Reaching for the chips, we drink, eat, and chat about nothing controversial or deep. The joy he finds in his family and friends is evident by the smile plastered across his face as he talks.

"Tell me about your family. I want to know all the deep, dark secrets," he chuckles.

"We are a normal family, I guess. My parents both work; my dad, step-dad actually, is in management at the local water and power company, and my mom works as assistant manager at the local picture studio. She loves kids and enjoys taking photos, so it was a great fit for her. My older sister lives with her boyfriend and is having a baby in five months. She seems happy, as far as I can tell," I respond. The wrinkle along Owen's forehead clues me in to his confusion.

"What is it?" I question, waiting for his gaze to meet mine. He takes another drink from his can then shifts his head toward the sky.

"You told me about your family, but you didn't tell me how you feel about them. It's like there is a disconnection in your life," he says.

"You're right. I don't feel a substantial connection to my family. I love my parents and my sister, but I have nothing in common with them. My parents did the best they could to take care of us. I played sports, took dance lessons, and got decent grades, but my family isn't terribly vocal when it comes to supporting each other. Sure, I got a pat on the back for a good report card or a game well played. Mom and Kevin, my step-dad, are proud of me, but they never had any huge hopes or dreams for me or Kendra, my sister. They never pushed me to try harder, to be smarter, to work longer, or to strive for my dreams. I'm not sure they have even asked me about my dreams," I say with brutal honesty.

"It sounds like that may be where your guy problems start. You want someone to fawn over you, treat you special, like you are the center of his universe because you have a gaping hole in your heart. Some parents aren't the greatest cheerleaders, but your parents sound like nice people, so don't hold this against them. But when the next guy comes knocking on your door, ask yourself if he's really what you want. Does he fill the hole in your heart to make you complete?" Owen drops his gaze from the sky and looks directly into my eyes. "We don't have to allow our past to define us or dictate the route of our future. That control is in our hands, ready for the taking. Don't ever forget that, Emma," he says without looking away.

"Thanks again for the chat, Dr. Phil," I say. Owen's face breaks into a smirk as I start laughing. "Time for one last warm beer," I proclaim loudly. We each flip the tab on our fresh beer cans and chug.

"So, change of subject. What's the deal with Tyler? I don't know him, but he seemed normal this morning. Then he went off the deep end in seconds. Is he always like that?" I ask.

"He's not a bad guy. Don't get me wrong—he can be an ass, but there's a lot going on with him at the moment. Apparently, he is self-medicating with alcohol, at least that's my impression of what happened today."

"Interesting," I say as my lip lifts at the corner.

"Why are you smiling? You enjoying somebody else's misery?" Owen chuckles.

"Here I've been having a pity party, thinking I'm the only person with issues, but it appears everyone is struggling with a problem or behavior or whatever. Knowing I'm normal is a bit of a mood-booster." I follow that comment with a chug of my unrefreshing beer.

"Don't be so down on yourself, Emma. What you don't realize is that while you are looking at the people surrounding you with envy, they in turn are looking back at you with their own envy. Have you always been oblivious to how others perceive you?" he asks. From the corner of my eye, I see him watching me. It feels like he made another back-handed compliment which is both intriguing and surprising. I'm not really sure what others see when they look at me.

"Your silence affirms my suspicion. Look at your life. I may not know you well, but I know this– you have a career that you enjoy and at which you appear to be rather successful. You have a college degree, a good group of friends, and a quiet confidence toward life. Maybe it's time you start recognizing all the good in you. It's ok to be proud of your accomplishments and your weaknesses. It's what makes us human. Picking the wrong type of guy or dating a bunch of men who are not up to par doesn't have to define your entire life. A giant kick in the ass is what you need so you wake up and see all the wonderful things about you." Owen exhales deeply as though he ran a marathon. "You have turned me into a Dr. Phil clone," he says, laughing.

The gravity of his comments weighs heavily on my mind and heart. I laugh along with him because I'm otherwise speechless and mindfully shocked. No man has ever said such nice things to me.

"Stop thinking, Emma, and just say thank you for my amazing psychoanalyzing skills," he says between laughs. Before I can respond, he has leaned over and started tickling my side below my ribcage. Laughter erupts from my lips as Owen continues his tickle assault with both hands. I try to defend myself, but he's much stronger than me, and I continue to fail at restraining one of his arms with both of mine. Between heavy breaths of laughter, I manage to strike, finding a sensitive spot beneath his arm pit. The tickles shock his body into a full-on offensive assault. My body is now pinned underneath him as he sits lightly upon my waist. Gathering both my wrists in one hand, he secures my arms above my head and continues a one-handed war on my body.

I'm gasping for air, trying to gain purchase of one of my arms with no success. The moon shines directly behind Owen's head, casting silver threads of light into his hair. The grip of his hands restraining me makes my heart flutter and my center throb. Slowly, the volume of my laughter quiets under Owen's gaze.

Like the shooting stars above, in a flash his lips are on my mine, evoking a brilliant display of desire throughout my core. And then his lips are gone. Thoughts spring through my mind faster than I can process. Chancing a look at Owen's face, I see his eyes warm and heavy with desire. His large body adjusts from a sitting position to blanketing me with the warmth of his skin. I search his eyes for answers and he responds in kind, lowering his head into the crook of my neck, his voice barely a whisper.

"You're a beautiful woman, Emma. Don't think. Let me worship your body like you deserve. No strings. No commitments or expectations." His lips ghost across the skin near my collarbone, the stubble on his face gently scraping across my neck. I am instantly flooded with longing. I respond to his statement physically, arching my body into his, raising my legs to cradle his body between them.

Owen's lips devour mine, his tongue making entry with gentle force. My fingers firmly grip his large biceps, pulling him closer. His hand cradles the side of my face as his lips retreat in surrender. My body writhes with the yearning pulsing through my core. I'm rewarded with Owen's hands gently running across my body while his lips mark the skin above my breasts. A shy moan escapes me as my sensitive nipple is freed from its restraint. Owen takes the pointed peak into his mouth with a gentle nip of his teeth, followed by the soothing wisp of his tongue. His touch is like nothing I have felt before. Each stroke of his hand and brush of his lips sends shocks straight to my heart.

Desire has voided all thoughts from my brain. With each gentle kiss and firm caress, my body responds with reckless abandon. My throbbing core seeks relief from the mounting desire. I'm not sure my body has ever responded to a man more fully than at this moment.

"Tell me you want this, Emma," Owen pleads while delicately kissing my face.

"I want this. I want you. But we don't have any protection," I say shyly, looking into his warm, hooded eyes.

"We will work it out," he responds before taking my mouth again.

My pelvis arches up into his leg, gently rubbing, trying to gain the friction it so desperately desires. Owen's hand replaces his leg, smoothly sliding the bottoms of my swim suit down and tossing them aside, his hand quickly covering my now bare sex. I gasp when his thumb presses into my button, igniting the bundle of nerves now spreading through my core, as a finger finds comfort deep inside me.

Owen's hand works my pussy with gentle precision while his mouth plunders my highly sensitive nipples. I'm completely lost in the moment, unaware of my surroundings as I allow my body to be played like a fine instrument. The pressure mounting deep inside me is evident as my walls grasp Owen's fingers with a greedy hunger.

My body soars over the edge when the stubble of Owen's beard finds my clit, sliding back and forth with a greedy rhythm. Another finger slides deep inside me as my body violently shudders and clenches in spectacular fashion. My thighs grip Owen's head with desperate need as he works the remainder of the orgasm from my rigid body. Consider this a mind blowing orgasm. An orgasm to end all orgasms.

A soft sheen covers my skin in reward. The

rhythm of my breath slows as my body falls limp into the sand below. Owen's now plump lips travel up my body as goosebumps spread across my limbs. Rolling to the side and propping himself on one elbow, Owen splays his hand across my chest with a smile.

"That was amazing, Emma," he says while lightly moving a strand of hair from my face.

"You were amazing. Now let me make you feel good too," I say quietly, unsure of myself. My hand presses firmly into the middle of his chest until his back lies firmly in the sand. I straddle his pelvis and begin my own assault of his body. I've never felt so confident with a man. So wanting. I gently tug his pert nipple with my teeth as my hands maneuver across the firm planes of his chest. With each caress of my hand his dick swells and hardens beneath me. Sitting up, I scoot back slightly so that I am resting between his legs and begin the delicate process of releasing his erection from its now tight confinement. Pushing away his trunks, I'm rewarded with the most stunning cock I have ever seen. I'm no expert, but this dick is a thing of beauty.

I begin working him slowly with my hand, admiring the pink skin and swollen head. Owen's eyes are plastered to my lips as I take his rock-hard cock into my mouth, running my tongue firmly along the bottom of the tip, while continuing to rub the base of his thick shaft with my hand. Taking Owen deeper into my mouth, my eyes remain locked with his. A hiss escapes his lips as I tighten my grip on his dick. "Faster!" he gasps. Full scale assault commences as I work Owen's penis with my mouth and hand. A frantic pace is set as I consume him like a jack hammer working a hole, driving harder and deeper until it shatters into a million pieces. Removing my mouth, I work the last bit of Owen's orgasm with my hand as his release shoots into the sand.

Quietly lying down beside him, I wrap my arm over his chest and settle my head into the crack between his body and arm. My mind is racing with pleasure. This man is amazing. He seems perfect – too good to even be true. I remind myself that tonight is a one-night stand. And that is perfectly acceptable to my life now. Consumed by pleasure, my breathing settles and my eyes close with a content smile on my lips as I drift into a peaceful slumber.

seven

A SHARP RAY OF SUN PEAKS OVER THE horizon as dawn breaks. My body is comforted by the warmth of Owen pressed firmly into my side. Gazing down, I realize I'm completely naked as the threat of daylight approaches. Delicately moving away from Owen, I grab the hastily tossed pieces of my bikini and slip them back into place. I sit quietly watching the birds awaken as the sun begins its ascent. Despite the circumstances, the beach is surrounded by stunning natural beauty and peace. The reeds sway gently in the delicate breeze that washes over the top of the water. A fish jumps near the mouth of the inlet while birds hunt from above.

My mind wants to race, to question my choices, chastise my decisions. But I heed Owen's advice and give myself a break. It's daylight, around 5am I would guess, as the sun is now rising. Somebody will come looking for us, or at worst, a fresh batch of boaters will appear, ending our unplanned camping trip. Quietly tip-toeing away from Owen's position, I walk along the water's edge allowing the sun to warm the slight chill covering my skin. The air is not cold by any means, but sleeping outside naked isn't exactly comfortable. Picking up a pebble from the beach, I skim it across the water.

What happened to Brandon? Only a complete asshole would leave his passengers behind to fend for themselves. It's not like we could Uber home from the middle of the lake. Never mind that there is limited signal strength on the south part of the lake as well. What was he thinking? Working myself into a frenzy isn't going to help the situation, so I continue walking, allowing the serene beauty to calm my nerves. I manage to climb around the tip of the inlet where a collection of large boulders have settled and sit myself down away from the water. There are no boaters at this time of morning, but it shouldn't be long before someone appears.

Movement over my shoulder alerts me to Owen's awakening. He's standing near our make-shift camp, stretching the kinks from his body. I give him a polite wave then return my gaze to the lake, willing a boat to appear. Minutes later, I hear the crunch of detritus under Owen's flip flops as he makes his way to where I sit. He takes a seat on a rock slightly below me.

"Any boaters out here yet?" he asks.

"None. But it can't be later than 5 or 6am, so I imagine we have another few hours before we are rescued," I say despondently.

"Probably," he answers.

"What do you think happened to Brandon?"

"I've been wondering that myself. There is no explanation that I can come up with that doesn't involve me causing him serious bodily injury once I get a hold of him," he says. The vein on the side of Owen's neck becomes more visible, as does the crease along his brow.

"This will all be over soon and we can forget it ever happened," I state, a yawn erupting from my lips.

"Yeah."

We sit in comfortable silence soaking in the sun's rays, watching the fish jump and the clouds soar across the dappled sky.

I hear buzzing coming from the north part of the lake, but when I glance that direction there is nothing in the water. Watching closely as the sound becomes more prominent, I see a white dot in the distance. Moments later, I recognize the shape as a boat. I tap Owen on the shoulder and point toward the small vessel heading our way.

"Looks like the park ranger," Owen comments confidently. We both stand in place as the boat comes into view, then we start waving our hands in greeting. I see what looks like an arm wave from the boat in response. "He sees us," I stammer in Owen's direction as I step carefully down and around my rocky perch. By the time I make it to the sand, the boat has arrived at the opening to the inlet and slowed to navigate its way onto the beach. I feel like an idiot, but I start jogging and waving at the park ranger as though I haven't seen another human for months.

The ranger dismounts the boat and gives us a friendly wave. "How you doing?" he asks. "Are you by chance Owen and Emma?"

"Yes, that's us," Owen responds quickly. "My buddy left us here last night. I'm going to tear his face apart when I get my hands on him," he chuffs.

The ranger's face droops for a moment before he takes a deep breath. "Is your friend Brandon? He has a passenger named Hailey, drives a very large boat with red graphics along the side?" He looks toward Owen.

"That's him. Did he send you out here to get us? That pussy couldn't face us himself?" I watch the vein that runs along Owen's temple pulse in anger.

The ranger frowns and begins, "There was a multi-boat accident about a mile north of here yesterday afternoon. By the time rescue services arrived on scene and handled the injured, a few hours had passed. Brandon was unconscious at the time, unable to speak. Hailey suffered a traumatic injury and was Medic-Vac'd out of here by helicopter. When your friends called in missing persons reports, we initially thought we had left two bodies out there in the water. Fortunately, Brandon regained consciousness and was able to inform us that you were not on the boat. He wasn't able to vocalize your whereabouts, so we had to sit tight until this morning to come out and look for you."

I'm rarely short on words, so I know I'm in shock when silence ensues. This scenario is all too familiar. Please, not again. The beating of my heart is so forceful, I fear it is going to explode from my chest.

"What happened? Are Brandon and Hailey going to be all right? Where is J?" Owen asks cautiously.

"Hailey was sliced across her hip by the propeller of another boat when it ran over the top of Brandon's vessel. The other driver was found to be impaired and is sitting in jail at the moment. From what I know, Hailey is in ICU and lost a ton of blood, but her condition is stable. Brandon was hit on the head by the same boat and suffered a moderate concussion as well as a dislocated shoulder. We didn't know about J until early this morning when we put all the pieces together. He's safe, having switched to another boat prior to the accident."

The air I've been holding in escapes with a large push. Relief fills my heart knowing Brandon, J, and Hailey are safe. We could have been on the boat as well. The afternoon hike turned out to be a stroke of luck.

"Let's get you back to town," the ranger says

before turning toward his boat. Owen and I shuffle along behind him, boarding the vessel and taking the only two seats remaining in the rear.

The ranger swiftly returns us to town in his small but steady boat. Owen has been feverishly texting since the moment his phone found a signal. When the ranger finally docks and helps us from the boat, I follow Owen along the dock to the marina office where I see Courtney and Ryan waiting for us under cover of the shaded patio.

Courtney hugs me desperately, as though I'm the last human on the planet. "I'm so sorry, Emma. This is all my fault. I encouraged you to go with Brandon. I haven't slept all night," she says, a few tears appearing at the corners of her eyes then trailing down her cheeks.

"It's not your fault," I tell her honestly. "We're fine," I say, gesturing between Owen and me. "I'm just grateful nobody was killed in the accident." I can hear Owen and Ryan chatting quietly when Tyler comes strolling out of the marina office with a donut and a cup of coffee.

I roll my eyes in his direction alerting him to my distaste at his presence.

"Hey, Emma. Sorry about yesterday. Getting

plastered in the middle of the day and starting a fight was dumb." Embarrassment colors Tyler's cheeks red at his admission.

"You have no reason to apologize to me, but thanks anyway," I say kindly. My stomach grumbles loudly before Tyler can respond. Courtney is staring at my belly in disbelief. "I'm hungry. I haven't eaten anything but a few chips and warm beer since lunch yesterday."

"Let's get you some breakfast," Courtney says then waves toward the parking lot. Grabbing me by the arm she tugs me close. "I was so worried...I..." Before she can apologize again, I interrupt.

"I'm fine. I don't want you to worry anymore. It's important to stay relaxed for the baby," I say with a smile.

"Did you have a hard time getting on the park ranger's boat?" Courtney's eyebrow raises slightly and a smirk drifts across her face.

"No, it was easy. Did you see how small it is? Total breeze. Stepped right in with no problem," I say confused.

"You weren't wearing a life vest when you pulled into the marina," she says quietly.

My mind freezes and so do my feet. A chill

quickly streaks through my entire body, pain grips my thundering heart. My breaths become short. How could I have forgotten to ask for a life vest? I'm surprised—shocked, really. During the entire ride to the marina, it never occurred to me that I was in danger. I felt comfortable, at ease even, despite the circumstances. Maybe the time has come to put my fear in the past. But is this really about fear? If I allow myself to move on then will I forget about my dad?

Of course, I didn't know my biological father well, but he's my dad and his loss had a profound effect on my life. The day of his accident I was four years old. My life vest is more than just my fear of boating. It's a reminder of my father. I know it's not rational to associate my life vest with a person, but it makes me feel safe, as though he is with me when I'm nervous, and boats definitely make me nervous.

My dad was a bit of a thrill-seeker. He loved anything with a motor and a little danger. Motorcycles, boats, cars. Anything that would go fast interested him. The day of his accident, we were at the boat races. My sister and I were in the pit area playing with the other kids, oblivious to the chaos happening on the water. At some point, we realized the noise from the races had ceased, and sirens were screaming from every direction. Dad's boat had been sideswiped by another racer resulting in both boats wrecking in a shocking display of destruction.

At the time of the crash, the boats were estimated to be traveling approximately seventy-five miles per hour. The hulls of the vessels skipped and slammed into the water, virtually destroying both. Dad was wearing the proper safety equipment, but the crash proved to be fatal. He drowned before rescue crews could pull him from the water.

Losing a parent when you are a child is a lifelong sorrow. We can accept the grief, the reality, but the wondering will never retreat. I wonder if he would have coached my softball team. Would he still be riding a motorcycle? Would he be proud of me? A million *woulds* have crossed my mind over the years. Dad would be proud that I survived last night and that I want to move forward from my drowning fear. I'm positive if Dad had survived the accident, he would have been back in his boat in due time. I've allowed my fear to cripple my confidence. It's like what Owen said to me last night - we can't allow our past to dictate our future. Moving forward doesn't mean we forget, it means we make the past a memory.

A strong grip on my shoulders pulls me from my thoughts. "What's going on, Emma?" Courtney asks quietly.

I smile. "It never occurred to me that I needed my life vest," I say, my eyes searching hers. She hugs me again and whispers in my ear, "I'm proud of you." Tears drip down my cheeks despite my happiness. Happy tears.

"Come on, the guys are waiting for us in the truck. We'll get you some clean clothes and some food," she, says tugging my arm to follow her.

The rest of the day is a peaceful blur. I take a shower and change then allow Courtney, Ryan, and Tyler to take me out to breakfast. I'm not sure where Owen went, but I don't see him again for the rest of the day.

Courtney and I decide boating is out of the question, so we set up camp on the beach just the two of us. Ryan and Tyler take the boat out by themselves for some guy time.

Sitting on the beach, relaxing in the sweltering heat of the sun, I acknowledge all the good that happened from this disastrous trip. I've come to terms with my mistakes and want to use them as building blocks for a better me. Owen helped me see that I'm more than my mistakes, and I can't thank him enough for his tender honesty.

I smile at the vision of Owen when we first met. Pegging him as a man-whore with narcissistic tendencies wasn't fair. He seemed like all the other guys I dated who were never really into me as a person. My mom tells me from time to time, *Don't be fooled by the masks we wear. Get to know the person on the inside first.* Who knew this trip would result in my transformation into a healthy adult – accepting my faults, vowing to change them, acknowledging my blessings.

I glance at my friend sitting next to me, our chairs in the water and cold drinks in our hands. My cup is overflowing. But not my disco ball tumbler, dammit. It sank with the rest of my things on Brandon's boat.

epilogue

THE DRIVE HOME SUNDAY FELT NEVER-ending. It seemed like at least a million mile markers raced by my window as Ryan drove us home. Apparently, we were all lost in thought. Before we left, Ryan was able to discover that Brandon was fully awake and assisting detectives with the crash investigation. Hailey lost a dire amount of blood, but her wounds will heal with time. The driver of the other boat was indeed legally drunk, his blood alcohol level above the legal limit for driving a motorized vehicle. Four passengers on his boat were uninjured but surely scarred for life. No drownings were reported at the lake for the entire weekend.

Courtney and I vowed to make more time for each other. She confided to me her crippling fears about being a mother Saturday night after Ryan and Tyler had gone to bed. Ryan doesn't comprehend the weight of her fears and is having a hard time supporting Courtney through this hiccup. I know Courtney will become a great mother, and Ryan is her biggest cheerleader, so that child will be blessed. Together they will work through her fears, becoming stronger in the process.

I return to work and my life as expected. Committed to enjoying the single life, I put myself first for the time being, consciously not looking for boyfriend material.

Owen crosses my mind frequently, always leaving a smile on my face. Who would have thought a one-night stand could be a positive, life-altering experience? I recall his tender caress and powerful kiss. I've considered getting Owen's phone number from Ryan but have refrained. Owen is the one who told me I deserve to be chased and cherished, to have somebody fall completely over me as I will eventually for him.

Falling over can be magical—if and when you

find the right person.

My phone dings, alerting me to an incoming text. I don't recognize the number but swipe to read the message anyway.

Unknown: *When can I see you again?*

Confused, I question if I should respond or ignore the wayward text. With a curious shrug I decide to respond.

Me: *Who is this?*

My heart thunders in my chest, an unexpected jolt of electricity shoots through my core as I wait for a response.

Unknown: *Owen*

Stunned, my heart flutters as my cheeks flush at the thought of him. His kind gestures, handsome face, and the way my body reacted to him as we lay stranded on the beach makes my body tingle with excitement. His response appears before me.

Unknown: *I'm Falling Over you*

The End.

If you enjoyed this novella, please consider leaving a review here: http://amzn.to/2pMwP8b

Note:

The idea for this novella came from a restless evening of picking up and setting down several books. I needed a different story. A story without billionaires, or down-and-out waitresses, or second chances. I yearned for a little depth, a lot of heart, and some mild heat. And I didn't want to be too invested in finishing the book. No all-night reading sessions, no trying to read while folding the laundry, and so on. What I needed was a one-night stand. A novel I could read whose story I could invest one good night and then be done, content. I have a few ideas for one-night stands. I hope you continue to follow along on this writing journey.

If you need a Disco Ball Tumbler in your life, and everyone does, check them out at the women-owned business, Packed Party.

www.packedparty.com
www.packedparty.com/shop/disco-drink

acknowledgements

Thank you to my editor and childhood friend, Lisa Murray, for believing in my writing (despite my terrible use of commas).

Matt Jones – thank you for supporting me as I travel along this writing journey. Your hard work allows me to make this dream a reality.

Leanne Swanson – I've often felt lonely in my life. Weird. I kept people at a distance, but you never let me push you away. And for that, I am eternally grateful. Thank you for supporting me when I couldn't support myself. Your time spent beta reading is priceless. I am the one who is honored with your friendship.

Rikki Johnson for keeping my social media filled with encouragement for tough girls. And pictures of Shane (see cover of Distorted).

Mary – Happy 40th Birthday. If not for your party, the awesome disco ball tumbler would not have made it into the text of this story.

Jenny – for graciously listening to me rant on occasion, because frankly, I'm a terrible people-person and without you, I would be a raging idiot.

Shep: Appreciate your time answering my nautical questions.

JoAnn, Terrie, Holly, Melissa, Jen I, Christina P, Connie and Mary from Love'n the Kitchen, and Pat Jones – your support and kind words mean the world to me.

Follow Me:

Facebook: www.facebook.com/Melodyjonesbooks

Website: www.melodyjonesbooks.com

Amazon: http://amzn.to/2pMwP8b

www.ingramcontent.com/pod-product-compliance
Lightning Source LLC
Chambersburg PA
CBHW070634130626
46555CB00006B/2545